W9-AZK-549

Karen's Haunted House

**Other books by
Ann M. Martin**

Leo the Magnificat
Rachel Parker, Kindergarten Show-off
Eleven Kids, One Summer
Ma and Pa Dracula
Yours Turly, Shirley
Ten Kids, No Pets
With You and Without You
Me and Katie (the Pest)
Stage Fright
Inside Out
Bummer Summer

THE BABY-SITTERS CLUB series
THE BABY-SITTERS CLUB mysteries
THE KIDS IN MS. COLMAN'S CLASS series
BABY-SITTERS LITTLE SISTER series
(see inside book covers for a complete listing)

BABY-SITTERS

Little Sister

Karen's Haunted House
Ann M. Martin

Illustrations by Susan Tang

A
LITTLE APPLE
PAPERBACK

SCHOLASTIC INC.
New York Toronto London Auckland Sydney

If you purchased this book without a cover, you should be aware that this book is stolen property. It was reported as "unsold and destroyed" to the publisher, and neither the author nor the publisher has received any payment for this "stripped book."

No part of this publication may be reproduced in whole or in part, or stored in a retrieval system, or transmitted in any form or by any means, electronic, mechanical, photocopying, recording, or otherwise, without written permission of the publisher. For information regarding permission, write to Scholastic Inc., Attention: Permissions Department, 555 Broadway, New York, NY 10012.

ISBN 0-590-06588-2

Copyright © 1997 by Ann M. Martin. All rights reserved. Published by Scholastic Inc. BABY-SITTERS LITTLE SISTER and LITTLE APPLE PAPERBACKS are trademarks and/or registered trademarks of Scholastic Inc.

10 9 8 7 6 5 4 3 2 1   7 8 9/9 0 1 2/0

Printed in the U.S.A.   40
First Scholastic printing, October 1997

The author gratefully acknowledges
Gabrielle Charbonnet
for her help
with this book.

1

Halloween Is Coming!

"Leaf monster! Leaf monster!" I yelled.

Hannie Papadakis squealed and leaped out of my way. I threw big handfuls of leaves into the air. "I am coming to get you!" I said with a growl.

Laughing, Hannie scooped up an armful of leaves and threw them back at me. I ran after her. It was not long before we both fell down into a big pile of leaves in the middle of her yard.

"You are a good leaf monster," said Han-

nie, panting. "Maybe you should be one for Halloween."

I am not always a leaf monster. Usually I am mild-mannered seven-year-old Karen Brewer, one of the Three Musketeers. (The other Musketeers are my two best friends, Nancy Dawes and Hannie.) We are all in Ms. Colman's second-grade class at Stoneybrook Academy.

But today I was also a leaf monster. It was October, and all the leaves on the trees had begun to change color and fall. The pile of leaves in Hannie's yard was gigundo. There were tons of yellow and red and orange leaves. It had taken her father all weekend to rake them up. Playing leaf monster had sort of spread them out again.

"You could glue leaves all over some long underwear," said Hannie. "No one would know who you are."

I giggled. "That is not a bad idea for a costume," I said. "But I have already decided to be Cinderella this year."

"Oh, cool," said Hannie.

"Yes. She is a blonde, beautiful princess," I said. "I am blonde too. It is perfect." (I do not know if Cinderella had blue eyes or freckles or wore glasses, like I do, but I do know we are both blonde. At least, she is blonde in the movie.)

"That will be a good costume," said Hannie. "I am probably going to be a butterfly. Mommy said she would help me with my costume. I want to have big wings that I can spread out." Hannie held out her arms to show me how big her wings would be.

"A butterfly would be great," I said. "But you know what? I wish we had something really special to do on Halloween."

"We will go trick-or-treating," said Hannie.

"I know, but — "

"And there will be the school parade on the Friday before Halloween," said Hannie.

"Yes," I said. "Those things will be fun. But I mean something *really* special. Maybe we could have a big party, at your house or my house. My big house, not my little house." (I will explain about my two houses in a minute.)

"Yeah," said Hannie. "We need to have a party."

"Or maybe we could go to a haunted house this year," I said. "Daddy said I was too young last year, but now I am seven. I would love to go to a haunted house." Being just a little bit scared is fun sometimes.

"A pretend haunted house, right?" asked Hannie. "Not a real one."

"Of course, a pretend one. I have seen signs for them," I said. "Where would we find a *real* haunted house?" I threw a couple of leaves at Hannie.

"I will tell you," said Hannie seriously. "Two doors down from here. Right on this street." (Hannie lives one door down and across the street from my dad.)

"What?" I said.

"Yes. That old house on the corner," said Hannie. "The people moved out a long time ago, and no one has bought it. It is falling to pieces. Probably it is haunted by now.

Maybe the people even moved out because it was haunted."

"I did not know that," I said. I knew which house Hannie was talking about. I have walked past it about a million times. The yard is full of tall weeds. Some of the windows are broken. It needs paint. It is missing some railings from its balconies. Now that I thought about it, it definitely looked haunted.

"I think you are right," I said. "I bet it is haunted now. That is too bad. It would be a pretty house if it was all fixed up."

"But no one will buy it and fix it up now," said Hannie. "Because it is haunted."

Big-House Halloween

"Please pass the ketchup," Sam said that night at dinner.

At the end of the table, Charlie tightened the cap on the ketchup. Then he tossed the bottle to Sam. Sam caught it.

"Enough of that," said Elizabeth sternly.

Who are these people? I bet you are wondering. They are the people in my family — my big-house family.

A long time ago, when I was little, I lived in just one house, the big house. In my family were me, Mommy, Daddy, and my little brother, Andrew. (He is four now, going on five.) Then Mommy and Daddy decided to get a divorce. Andrew and I moved with Mommy to the little house, not far away. Daddy stayed in the big house. (It is where he grew up.) Now Andrew and I switch houses every month. We stay at the big house for a month, then at the little house for a month.

When we are at the little house, we live with Mommy and Seth Engle, who is our stepfather. Also at the little house are Midgie, Seth's dog, and Rocky, Seth's cat. Plus Bob, Andrew's pet hermit crab, and Emily Junior, my pet rat. (Bob and Emily Junior go back and forth with Andrew and me.) The little house has a little-house-sized family.

But the big house has a big-house-sized family! Daddy got married again too, to Elizabeth Thomas. Elizabeth already had four kids. They are Sam and Charlie, who are in high school; Kristy, who is thirteen and the best stepsister ever; and David

Michael, who is seven like me. He goes to Stoneybrook Elementary.

And there are more big-house people. There is also Emily Michelle, who is two and a half. Daddy and Elizabeth adopted her from a country called Vietnam. (I love her, so I named my pet rat after her.) And there is Nannie, who is Elizabeth's mother. She came to help take care of all the people and the pets.

The big-house pets (besides Bob and Emily Junior) are Boo-Boo, Daddy's old cat; Shannon, David Michael's humongous puppy; and Goldfishie and Crystal Light the Second. If you guessed they are goldfish, you are right.

Now you know who all the people are at the dinner table. There are so many of us that we eat at a long, long table with two long, long benches. I like to sit next to Kristy. I do not like to sit next to Emily Michelle. She throws food.

Daddy tapped his spoon against his water glass. "I have some news," he said. "Mrs.

Porter's daughter and granddaughter are moving back in with her. I think they will stay for good this time."

I felt Kristy looking at me. Mrs. Porter is our next-door neighbor. Daddy calls her Mrs. Porter, but she has another name too: Morbidda Destiny. That is her witch name. Everyone knows that I know that Morbidda Destiny is a witch. But they do not let me talk about it.

A while ago, Morbidda's daughter, Mrs. Peterson, and *her* daughter, Druscilla, came to stay with Morbidda. They came because Druscilla's parents were getting a divorce. Then they moved to their own apartment. Now they were coming back. I will tell you something. Druscilla is my age, and I think she is a witch-in-training. The last time I saw her, she said she was not a witch. Since then I realized that this does not mean she is not a witch-in-training. It just means she is not yet an actual witch. So there you go.

"Karen, I am expecting you and Hannie

and Nancy to be nice to Druscilla," said Daddy. "She will need friends."

I ate a french fry. "Okay, Daddy," I said. "Will she be going to Stoneybrook Academy?" It would be weird to have a witch-in-training in Ms. Colman's second-grade class.

"I do not think so," said Daddy. "I believe she will go to Stoneybrook Day School like she did before."

I tried not to look too relieved.

"Hey!" said Charlie. "Who drank the last of the milk?"

"You snooze, you lose," said Sam.

"Milk hog!" said Charlie. "What did you do, take a bath in it?"

"There is more milk in the fridge," said Daddy firmly.

"Taking a bath is an idea you might try sometime, Charlie," said Sam, holding his nose. "You might try changing your socks too."

"Okay, boys, enough," said Elizabeth in

her no-nonsense voice. "Charlie, please get more milk from the fridge. Sam, no more personal comments."

For a few moments everyone was quiet. I knew it would not last. Quiet never lasts long at the big house. That is what I like about it.

Hannie's Surprising Announcement

"School, school, school," I sang as I hopped off the school bus. Hannie hopped off right behind me. When I am at the big house, I ride the school bus with Hannie. At the little house I ride the school bus with Nancy, since she lives next door. I am lucky to live so close to both of my best friends.

"Hi!" Nancy called. She waved us over to a hopscotch area she had saved. We played hopscotch until the bell rang and it was time for school to start.

My friends and I hurried to our classroom. I went to my desk in the very first row. I sit there because I wear glasses. (Blue ones for reading, and pink ones the rest of the time.) My pretend husband, Ricky Torres, sits next to me on one side. Natalie Springer sits on my other side. We all wear glasses. Guess what. Ms. Colman, our gigundoly wonderful teacher, wears glasses too.

Hannie and Nancy sit in the last row, next to each other. I used to sit with them, before I got glasses. But I see better up front.

"Good morning, class," said Ms. Colman cheerfully. "Karen, could you take attendance, please?"

"Yes! Oh, boy," I said, leaping out of my chair. I love taking attendance. It is a very important job. I got the attendance book and a pen from Ms. Colman. Then I looked at her list.

"Tammy and Terri Barkan," I read. "Check, check." They are twins. "Me, check. Nancy Dawes, check. Sara Ford, Bobby Gianelli, check, check." (Bobby used to be the class bully. But he is not so bad anymore.) "Jannie Gilbert, Audrey Green, Pamela Harding" (Pamela is my best enemy). "Omar Harris, Ian Johnson . . . " Hmm. Ian was absent. I put a big X next to his name. "Chris Lamar, Leslie Morris, Hannie Papadakis, Hank Reubens, Addie Sidney, Natalie Springer, Ricky Torres." I handed the attendance book back to Ms. Colman and sat down.

"Thank you, Karen," said Ms. Colman.

"Oh, Ms. Colman!" said Hannie. She waved her hand. "I have an announcement to make."

"All right," said Ms. Colman. "Please come to the front of the class."

Hannie stood in front of us and held up a poster. It said HALLOWEEN HAUNTED HOUSE/HOMES FOR FAMILIES.

"My parents are going to make a haunted house for Halloween," said Hannie. "It will be in an empty house on our block."

I gasped, and Hannie grinned at me.

"The city owns the house now," contin-

15

ued Hannie. "And the mayor said we could use it. My parents are asking different groups to sign up to decorate the house. Each group will work on one room. They will make the rooms look as spooky as they can. Then, on Halloween, Homes for Families will charge admission to the house. After Halloween, Homes for Families will use the money to help fix up the house for families who cannot afford to buy a place to live in."

"That is a wonderful idea, Hannie," said Ms. Colman.

"My parents wanted to know if our class would like to sign up to decorate a room in the haunted house," said Hannie. "We could work after school and on weekends."

"What do you think, class?" asked Ms. Colman. "Would you like to make a spooky room in a haunted house? It sounds like fun."

"I want to!" I cried, waving my arm around.

"I want to too," said Ricky Torres.

"Me too," said Addie Sidney.

"Okay, let's take a vote," said Ms. Colman.

The vote was unanimous. (That means everyone voted the same way.)

"I will make permission slips at lunchtime," said Ms. Colman. "And we can start a sign-up sheet. Fill in your name and the afternoons when you are available to work on the house. I will also talk to Mr. and Mrs. Papadakis and find out all the details on what we need to do."

Hannie sat down at her desk, smiling happily. I turned around and gave her the thumbs-up sign. What a great announcement, I thought. I wiggled in my seat. I could not wait to start decorating our spooky haunted-house room!

4

The Return of Druscilla

That afternoon Nancy came home with Hannie and me. (She had called her mother for permission.) After Nannie fixed us a snack, the three of us sat in my front yard.

"The house has twelve rooms," said Hannie. "They will all be decorated."

"Even the bathrooms?" asked Nancy.

"Yes," said Hannie. "Plus the hallways and everything. Mommy has talked to a million people. There are some groups from the hospital who will help. And people from our church have volunteered. The people

19

who work at the grocery store have said they will do a room."

"Gosh," I said. "Are we the only kids?"

Hannie shook her head. "No. Mommy is going to ask kids from Stoneybrook High School. I bet some of them will want to help."

"Sam and Charlie go to Stoneybrook High," I said. "I hope they sign up to decorate."

"Hi!" said a voice from over the hedge.

Hannie, Nancy, and I all jumped. Then Druscilla Peterson poked her head around the end of the hedge.

"Oh, hi, Druscilla," I said. "Come on over. Daddy told me you were moving back." (I had already told the other two Musketeers about that.)

Now, if you have never met a witch-in-training (W.I.T.), you might not be able to recognize one. But Druscilla is easy to spot. For one thing, she has wild black hair. She also dresses all in black, all the time. (Once she told me it was because black matches everything, but I am not stupid. I saw through that.) She also eats weird foods, such as mushroom sandwiches. I am not making that up.

But the last time Druscilla stayed with Morbidda Destiny — I mean Mrs. Porter — I got to know her. She is not that bad. She is just different.

Now Druscilla sat with us. She wore black leggings and a long black sweater. Her hair was fixed in two neat braids, tied with black bows.

"I love autumn," she said, sniffing the air. Her nose wiggled. "I smell leaves burning and food cooking. Everything is so crisp and clean."

"I like autumn too," I said. "It is the start of all the holidays. And the trees look so pretty."

"Speaking of holidays," said Hannie, "we were just talking about Halloween. My parents are organizing a haunted house."

"Cool," said Druscilla.

Just then Mrs. Porter came up our walk.

She has frazzly gray hair, and dresses all in black, like Druscilla. She has "witch" written all over her.

"Hello, girls," she said with a smile. "Are you enjoying this beautiful weather?"

"Yes," said Hannie politely. "I was just telling Druscilla about my parents' Halloween haunted house. It will be in the old abandoned house at the end of our block. We will decorate it — "

"Oh, no!" cried Mrs. Porter. "Not the old Powell house!"

"Um, yes," said Hannie.

"Oh, but you cannot!" said Mrs. Porter.

Hannie, Nancy, and I stared at her.

"Why not?" asked Nancy.

"Because there are bats living in the chimney," said Mrs. Porter. "Every night at dusk, the bats swarm out. I always watch them. It is a wonderful sight. If the house is disturbed, the bats will have nowhere to live. Someone must save the bats," she said firmly.

Well, my mouth dropped open. Save the

bats? Yuck. Double yuck! Only Morbidda Destiny would want to save some yucky, spooky, icky old bats. If I ever needed proof that she was a witch, here it was.

"I must talk to your parents about this," said Mrs. Porter. "Druscilla, dinner will be in an hour."

"Okay," said Druscilla.

After Mrs. Porter left, I did not know what to say. Just thinking about yucky bats made me feel shivery. I looked up at the sky. It was starting to get dark. I did not see any bats.

"I am sure Mommy and Daddy will come up with a way to deal with the bats," said Hannie. "I am sure we will have the haunted house."

"Yes," I agreed. "Druscilla, you should come over and help us. You must know a lot about haunted houses."

"Why?" asked Druscilla.

"Well, you know," I said. I did not want to come right out and say I knew she was a W.I.T. She was probably trying to keep it quiet. "I bet you have a lot of neat stuff lying around — creepy stuff that we could use. Spooky stuff."

Druscilla's eyes narrowed. Her nose wiggled. "I just have regular stuff," she said.

"Oh, sure," I said. I winked at her.

Druscilla rolled her eyes. "I better go unpack before dinner," she said. She got up and walked across the grass to Mrs. Porter's yard.

"What?" I asked Hannie and Nancy. "What did I say?"

Hannie and Nancy shrugged.

"I guess she is just sensitive about witch stuff," said Nancy. "Do not worry about it. You were trying to be nice."

But I did worry about it. It is not good to be on the bad side of a witch. Even a witch-in-training.

5

Spooky Plans

On Saturday morning I ran to the abandoned house right after breakfast. Mrs. Papadakis was standing on the front porch, holding a clipboard. I would have been scared if I had not seen her. The house already looked spooky and creepy to me. Shutters sagged on their hinges. Vines grew up the outside of the house. It was perfect for Halloween!

"Good morning, Karen," said Mrs. Papadakis. "Ms. Colman's class has been assigned one of the upstairs bedrooms. Some

25

of your classmates are already here."

"Thank you," I said. I stepped through the front door. Inside, the house did not look quite as scary. Mostly it just needed cleaning and painting. I saw a big staircase on the left, and I climbed it. It squeaked. I thought about the bats living in the chimney, and I shivered. I hoped they would not come out while I was there.

Upstairs, many people were walking around. There were grown-ups from different groups, and lots of older kids. Both Sam's and Charlie's high-school homerooms had signed up to help, but my brothers were not there yet.

At the end of the hall, a door stood open. I saw Ms. Colman through it.

"Hello, Karen," she said. "You are just in time. We are taking suggestions for decorating ideas."

The other two Musketeers were there. So were Terri and Tammy, Audrey, Chris, Bobby, Ricky, Pamela, and Sara. Ms. Colman held a notebook.

26

"I will write down our ideas," she said. "Then we will decide which ones we like best."

Our room faced the front yard. It had two windows and a fireplace. (I hoped there were no bats inside it.) A broken mirror hung over the fireplace. I saw a big closet. Flowered paper covered the walls. The wooden floor was scratched and dirty.

"Let's paint the walls black," called out Bobby.

"Let's put a spiderweb over the mirror," I said.

"Rip some of the wallpaper," said Audrey.

"Hang more spiderwebs from the chandelier," suggested Hannie.

"Paint some skeletons on the walls," I said.

"Put spooky pumpkins in the windows," said Pamela.

Ms. Colman quickly wrote down our ideas. "All of these are very good suggestions," she said. "I will need to make a list of supplies to buy. In the meantime, we could begin taking down some of this wallpaper."

Usually kids have to be careful not to mess up the walls. Parents do not want fingerprints or dirt or scratches all over everything. But in this house, the worse it looked, the better. So we started ripping off wallpaper! It was so much fun. We made a gigundo mess.

Outside our door, I heard people talking loudly. Sam and some of his friends were standing in the hallway.

"Sophomores rule!" Sam said loudly. His arms were crossed over his chest.

Down the hall stood Charlie and a bunch of *his* friends. "Sopho-*mores* should be called sopho-*less*," said Charlie. Some of his friends laughed. "Everyone knows seniors are best. We are going to have the scariest room in the house."

"No, *we* are," said Sam. "Seniors are scared of everything. You will not know how to decorate your room."

"Look who is talking," said Charlie.

Just then their teachers came into the hall.

They made Sam's group go into Sam's room, and Charlie's group go into Charlie's room. I went back into Ms. Colman's room.

Sam and Charlie were so silly sometimes. Lately it seemed as if they argued about everything.

I gathered up a huge pile of torn wallpaper and stuffed it into a trash can. The room already looked awful! Our room was going to be *much* spookier than Sam's or Charlie's!

6

Let the Decorating Begin!

On Sunday our class met again at the haunted house. (Not everyone could be there.) Ms. Colman had brought some gray and black paint and other supplies.

Several groups worked in their rooms. A group from the hospital had chosen one of the downstairs rooms. They had already started to paint the room black.

The people from the grocery store were in charge of the front yard. They had left most of the weeds there, and they were putting in fake tombstones. The yard would look like a creepy graveyard when they were finished.

Sam's class would not let anyone look in their room. But I saw them carrying in buckets of red paint and a pile of white sheets. I hoped their room would not be *too* scary.

Charlie's room was going to be one gigundoly huge spiderweb. The whole house shook as they hammered in long black ropes from wall to wall.

By Sunday afternoon I was pretty tired. We had been slopping black and gray paint all over the walls. It did not matter if we spilled it on the floor. I had paint speckles all over me. But our room looked awful! And it was going to get worse!

"Please pass the skull stencil," said Addie. She rolled her wheelchair closer to the wall. It was Tuesday afternoon after school, and our haunted-house room was beginning to look pretty haunted. (So far I had not seen any bats. Thank heavens.) Some of the high-school boys had carried Addie and her wheelchair up the stairs. Now she was painting the lower stencils, and other kids were painting the higher stencils.

Our class had decided on a "skeleton party" theme. We had painted everything gray and black. The walls looked creepy, like old walls from a haunted mansion. Now we were painting white skeletons and skulls and other bones on the walls. We were using stencils that Ms. Colman had bought. Some of the stencils were taller than I am.

Hannie and I taped our stencil to the wall. Then Hannie held some of the edges while I sponged white paint over the stencil. When we carefully took it off, *voilà*! A tall, dancing skeleton grinned eerily at us.

"These things really work," said Hannie.

"I am glad they do not scare Jane," I said.

Jane is Ms. Colman's baby daughter. Ms. Colman had brought her to the house this afternoon. Jane sat in her infant carrier in the middle of the room. She was enjoying watching us work. The skeletons did not seem to bother her at all. She clapped her

hands and laughed a lot. She must be a very brave baby.

"Oops, my dad is here," said Hank. He put his stencil down on our worktable. "See you guys tomorrow morning at school."

"'Bye, Hank," we all said.

One by one our classmates left to go home for dinner. Nancy had to go home too. Since Hannie and I lived right down the street, we could stay a little later.

Soon just the two of us and Ms. Colman and Jane were in our room. It was practically dark outside. The dingy chandelier overhead glowed with a dim light. I held a stencil while Hannie painted. (We were taking turns.)

"I need to discuss something with Mrs. Papadakis," said Ms. Colman. "If you need me, I will be downstairs."

"Okay," said Hannie. "We will start to put our things away."

Ms. Colman picked up Jane's infant carrier and left the room. I began putting caps back on cans. We put our paint sponges in plastic bags so we could use them again. Hannie laid the stencils carefully on the worktable so they would dry.

All of a sudden I felt the little hairs on the back of my neck rise up. I looked around. It was dark outside, almost dinnertime. The house seemed very quiet.

"Hannie, has everyone else gone home?" I asked.

Hannie listened for a moment. "It sounds like it," she said. "I do not hear anyone else."

I walked to the door and looked down the hall. It was dark and empty. Although Mrs. Papadakis and Ms. Colman were right downstairs, upstairs seemed very creepy and lonely.

"Come on, Hannie," I said. "Let's get out of here."

Hannie and I were heading for the staircase when suddenly — "*Awooo, awooo.*" We heard a loud, scary howling sound! It sounded like a pack of wolves! I grabbed Hannie's hand. Her eyes were big. She looked about as scared as I felt. Then, *wham!* A door slammed down the hall. But no one else was upstairs.

"This house really *is* haunted," I whispered.

7

Save the Bats

"How did the decorating go today?" asked Elizabeth.

"Great," said Sam.

"Terrific," said Charlie.

I spooned some lima beans onto my plate. (Not too many. I am not crazy about lima beans.)

"Karen?" asked Elizabeth.

"Um, fine," I said. I took a sip of milk.

After Hannie and I had heard the howling and the door slamming, we had screamed and run downstairs. Outside we had found

Ms. Colman and Mrs. Papadakis standing on the front porch going over our schedule.

"Girls! What is wrong?" asked Ms. Colman.

Hannie and I looked at each other. Now that we were outside, with grown-ups, it seemed pretty silly to say that we had heard weird noises. So we just shrugged. Then Sam walked through the front gate.

"Hey, Karen," he said. "Are you ready to go home? I told Mom I would walk you and Hannie if it was dark."

Since then I had thought some more about what Hannie and I had heard. We had both heard it. I had not imagined it by myself. (I have a big imagination.)

"Has anyone ever heard of a real haunted house?" I asked. "I mean, could the house on the corner really be haunted?"

My big-house family laughed.

"You wish, Karen," said Charlie. "Then Morbidda Destiny could move in there, instead."

"Her name is Mrs. Porter," Daddy said sternly.

"Karen, you are such a kidder," said Kristy. She smiled at me. "You really know how to enjoy a holiday, especially Halloween."

I smiled weakly. But I had not been kidding. I was starting to worry about the haunted house.

"Speaking of Mrs. Porter," said Daddy, "she has begun a save-the-bats campaign."

"Eww," I said. I wrinkled my nose.

"The city has had a pest-control company examine the bats," said Daddy. "They are clean and free of diseases. So we have two choices: Either exterminate them, or listen to Mrs. Porter. She wants people to put up bat houses in their yards. Then when the bats are chased out of the haunted house, they will be able to find new homes."

"I do not think they should be exterminated," said Elizabeth. "They have not done any harm."

"But no one wants a bat house in their yard," I said. "Who would want a yucky creepy bat living so close by? It is just like Morbidda Destiny to come up with such a witchy plan. I bet once people have bats in their yard, Morbidda will use them to cast spells — "

"Karen, would you like to be excused?" asked Daddy.

"No," I mumbled.

"Bats are not bad," said Elizabeth. "They are actually very good for the environment. They eat tons of insects. That means we can use fewer pesticides."

"Bats pollinate plants and scatter seeds," said Daddy. "Just like birds and bees do."

"Bats are kind of cute," said Kristy.

I stared at her.

"I think Mrs. Porter is right," said Daddy. "I think we should try to save the bats. Tomorrow I will buy some bat houses for our yard."

I wondered where he could get a bat house. Bats 'R' Us?

"Good idea," said Elizabeth. "I have seen bat houses at the gardening store."

Oh.

"They will help keep the mosquitoes and flies from bothering us in the summer," said Nannie.

Next summer is a long way away, I wanted to say. But I did not. I wanted to say that we did not need any yucky flying-rat bats in our yard. I wanted to say that this was just a bad, witchy plan. But I kept my mouth shut. I did not want to be sent to my room. Not when we were having apple pie for dessert.

8

Prime Suspect

"No, no, Natalie," I said on Wednesday afternoon. "These are supposed to be *spooky* skeletons." Natalie Springer kept trying to paint nice smiles on the skeletons in our room at the haunted house. I had to watch her like a hawk.

"But they are at a party," said Natalie. She leaned over and pulled up her socks. "They should be having a good time."

"They are having a *spooky* time," I told her. "They are at a *haunted* party. They should not look too friendly."

"Karen is right," said Nancy. "We are trying to make our room look scary. Cheerful skeletons are not what we need."

"For once I agree with Loudmouth Karen," said Pamela. "Make our skeletons mean-looking."

I narrowed my eyes at Pamela. I wanted to say, Just make them look like Pamela. But I could not, because she had agreed with me. (Although she had called me a loudmouth.)

"Okay, okay," said Natalie. "I will make them look mean."

I stood back and looked around at our room. We had made a lot of progress. There were still many things left to do, though. On Halloween night we planned to have a refreshments table covered with yucky, spooky skeleton food. We would serve witch's brew, and worm-covered mud pies, and rotten apples. We would play scary music on a hidden tape player. Ms. Colman was going to make a game and hang it on the wall. It would be Pin the Skull on the Skeleton.

Our room was going to be fabulous.

"Pamela, your mother is honking her horn out front," said Ms. Colman.

So Pamela and Jannie Gilbert left. Then Chris Lamar left. And so did Tammy and Terri. Soon it was just me, Hannie, Nancy, and Ms. Colman.

"Have we put skeletons in the closet yet?" asked Ms. Colman. "We want them to jump out when someone opens the door."

"Bobby was working on it," I said. "Let me check." I walked over to the closet and opened the door. A huge, hairy spider leaped out at my face! Its awful little legs scrambled against my hair!

"*Aiieegghh!*" I screamed, batting at it. "Get it off, get it off!"

Hannie and Nancy ran to me. I was spinning in a circle, clawing at my hair.

"Hold still," cried Nancy.

"Get it off!" I yelled.

"Okay," said Hannie. She peered at my hair. "Oh. It is plastic."

"Whaaaat?" I shrieked.

"It is a fake spider," said Nancy, picking it out of my hair. She showed it to me.

"Get it off, get it off!" said a high-pitched voice from inside the closet. Bobby Gianelli stepped out of the darkness, laughing. "That was great!" he said loudly. "You should have seen your face!" He pretended to pat his hair, jumping up and down and squealing.

I put my hands on my hips. "Bobby, that was not funny," I said angrily. "Playing tricks is mean."

"Besides, we have too much work to do to play tricks," said Ms. Colman. "Now, I think your mother just arrived. Please do not play any more tricks."

"Okay," said Bobby. But he grinned as he walked past me.

"Boys are so stupid sometimes," I said. My cheeks burned. I had screamed and jumped around. But the spider really had been gross. I shuddered again, just thinking about it crawling on my hair. (It had not really crawled. But it had *felt* like it.) And what if it had been a real spider? Or a bat?

I sighed. "I am ready to go home now too."

Ms. Colman turned off our light and closed the door to our room. Hannie, Nancy, Ms. Colman, and I started to walk toward the stairs. The hallway was empty and dark. Then a spooky laugh floated down from the ceiling. *"Ha-ha-ha-ha-ha-haaaaaa!"* It sounded just like a ghost laughing.

We stopped where we were. I looked up, but did not see anything. Ms. Colman said, "Bobby?"

There was no answer.

Another door opened, and Charlie and some of his classmates stepped out into the hall.

"What was that?" asked Charlie. "Did you guys hear something?"

"It is just someone playing a trick," said Ms. Colman calmly. "Come, girls. Let's go downstairs." With Ms. Colman leading the way, Hannie and Nancy and I slunk downstairs, looking over our shoulders the whole time.

* * *

I asked Elizabeth if I could call Hannie that night after dinner. She said I could.

"Hannie, what is going on with the haunted house?" I said.

"I do not know," said Hannie. "It is very creepy. I wish we did not have to go back."

"But we do," I said. "Our room is not finished."

"Maybe it was Bobby again," said Hannie. "It probably was."

An idea came to me in a flash. "Maybe it was Druscilla," I said. "Maybe she is trying to get back at me for what I said. Did you notice how her nose twitched the other day?"

"Um, no," said Hannie.

"Well, it did. Just like the witch on that old TV show. Her nose twitched whenever she cast a spell. Now *Druscilla's* nose is twitching, and the haunted house is really haunted. It is very clear to me."

"Hmm," said Hannie.

"We have to get to the bottom of this," I said. "We cannot be chased out of our own haunted house."

"You are right," said Hannie. "But how?"

"I will think of something," I said.

9

Dueling Cinderellas

On Friday afternoon I did not go to the haunted house to decorate. Kristy and Charlie had offered to take me to Pembroke's Party Store downtown. It is a very cool store with all kinds of things for holidays. They have costumes too.

"Hurry up, Karen," said Kristy. "I have a Baby-sitters Club meeting soon."

Kristy and a bunch of her friends run a baby-sitting business. She goes to meetings three times a week.

"Okay, I will hurry," I said. Since I was going to be Cinderella, I planned to look through Pembroke's princess supplies.

At Pembroke's I found some clear plastic slippers that looked like real glass. I also found a silky cape with white fake fur around the edges. It was perfect. (I already had a fancy dress at home.)

I bought those things, and Charlie drove us home.

"I am going to be a great Cinderella," I told Kristy as Charlie parked in our driveway. "I have the right hair color. And Elizabeth is helping me with the fancy ball gown. It is an old dress of hers that she is shortening for me. It is shiny and blue and silky — "

"Hello," called Druscilla. She had just gotten out of her grandmother's car and was running up her walk. She was carrying a bag that said PEMBROKE'S PARTY STORE on it.

I remembered that I should be nice, even though she might have been haunting our haunted house lately. Maybe if I was friendly, Druscilla would quit making spooky things happen.

"Hello," I said. "Were you at Pembroke's? We must have just missed each other." I held up my own bag.

"Yes," said Druscilla. She sneezed and wiped her nose with a tissue. "Pembroke's is a neat place. I got everything I need for my Halloween costume."

"Oh? What are you going to be?" asked Kristy.

"Cinderella," said Druscilla.

Well, for heaven's sake.

"Cinderella!" I cried. "Why are you going to be Cinderella?"

Druscilla looked at me. "I *like* Cinderella," she said. "I have been planning my costume for weeks."

"But you cannot be Cinderella!" I said. "I am going to be Cinderella. It was my idea."

Druscilla shrugged. "I had the same idea."

"There is no reason why you cannot both be Cinderella," said Kristy.

"We cannot be the same thing," I said, putting my hands on my hips. "Anyway, you are not blonde. Cinderella was blonde. I say, whoever is naturally blonde should get to be Cinderella."

"That is silly," said Druscilla. "Who said that Cinderella was blonde?"

I felt as if my eyes were about to pop out of my head. "The movie!" I shrieked. "In the movie, Cinderella is blonde!"

"Well, I have read other books," said Druscilla. "And in some of the books, Cinderella has dark hair. Walt Disney did not make up the story of Cinderella."

My mouth dropped open.

"I still think you can both be Cinderella," said Kristy.

"No, we cannot!" I said. "I was first, Druscilla. You should take back your costume." I had forgotten all about being nice to the W. I. T.

"No," said Druscilla. Her nose twitched, and she sneezed again. "You take yours back if you don't like it."

54

"I will not!" I said. I stamped my foot. I had planned a gigundoly wonderful costume, and Druscilla was ruining everything. Just like a witch. "And another thing," I said. "I know you have been playing tricks at our haunted house. You are just a meanie-mo."

"Karen!" said Kristy.

"I have not been playing tricks!" said Druscilla. "I would not go near that haunted house if you paid me."

"Sure," I said sarcastically.

"You are crazy," said Druscilla. She wiped her nose again with a tissue and headed up her front steps. "I am going to be Cinderella, and there is nothing you can do about it."

She slammed her front door. I stamped my foot again.

"Now you have done it," said Kristy. "Karen, you were very rude to Druscilla. Go on inside. I am going to my meeting."

"She started it," I grumbled. I knew that was not true. I also knew that Druscilla was going to ruin my Halloween.

10

Really and Truly Haunted

"Listen to that wind," said Nancy.

"It is good weather for decorating our room," said Ms. Colman.

Rain splashed against the bedroom windows at the haunted house. It was a dreary, drizzly, autumn Saturday. Ms. Colman was right: It was good weather for decorating our room.

This morning Hannie and Nancy and I had walked through all the rooms of the haunted house. It was just about the spookiest house I had ever seen. The front yard was full of weeds and tombstones. Someone had put a green skeleton hand in the dirt by one of the tombstones. It looked as if it were reaching up out of the ground. Yuck!

Inside, the first thing you saw was a coffin propped against the wall. It was partly open. Another skeleton hand stuck out of it. There were spiderwebs everywhere, with big plastic spiders hanging in them. Black rubber rats perched on fireplace mantels. The floors were dusty. Walls were painted black and gray. They were cracked and chipped down to the plaster.

I had never seen such a scary haunted house. And this was during the *daytime*.

Our room upstairs was almost finished. I was taping an old tattered sheet to our worktable. It would be the tablecloth for the skeleton-party refreshments. We had sprinkled it with red and black paint. Since the weather was so icky, many of my classmates had not come to work on the house today. Chris and Ian had been here earlier, but had already gone home. Now it was just the

Three Musketeers and Ms. Colman.

Mrs. Papadakis stuck her head into our room. "Gee, this room looks great, girls."

"Thank you, Mommy," said Hannie.

"You all have worked really hard," said Mrs. Papadakis. "I cannot wait to see this room on Halloween night."

"It might be *too* scary," said Nancy.

Mrs. Papadakis laughed. "The scarier it is, the more people will like it. Ms. Colman, could you come downstairs for a moment? I'd like to go over some plans with you."

"Certainly," said Ms. Colman. "You girls will be all right up here, won't you?"

"Um, sure," I said. I did not want to look like a baby. As soon as they left, a big streak of lightning lit our room, and thunder shook the house.

Hannie shivered. "Let's finish up and get out of here," she said. "This place is giving me the creeps."

"Me too," said Nancy.

"Me three," I said with a grin. Because we are the Three Musketeers — get it?

We began to put our art supplies away. When I had to put something in the closet, I quickly flung open the door and jumped back. No spiders leaped out at me.

Ha, Bobby, I thought. I am too smart for you.

We turned off the light to our room and shut the door behind us. In the hallway, large wispy spiderwebs floated from the light fixtures. A spooky witch peeked out from a doorway. Red lightbulbs glowed overhead.

Downstairs we heard doors slamming. It could have been Ms. Colman or Mrs. Papadakis. Then the howling started! It was that same creepy howl I heard before: "*Awooo, awoooo!*" It seemed to be coming from all directions at once. Hannie and Nancy and I grabbed hands.

When the door beside us flew open, I screamed, "*Aiiieeee!*"

"Karen!" said Sam. "What is the matter? Who was howling?"

Hannie, Nancy, and I were clumped together in the hall, holding tightly to each other.

"I do not know," I whispered.

The eerie howling surrounded us again. *"Awooo, awoooo!"*

"Where is Charlie?" I said shakily. I would feel safer if both Sam and Charlie were with us.

"He went home about ten minutes ago," said Sam. "I am going to find out who is doing this. Come on, guys." Sam and several of his classmates trooped down the stairs loudly. The Three Musketeers ran after them. We wanted to stay with the big kids.

Ms. Colman and Mrs. Papadakis were in the front hallway. They had heard the noises too.

"Are you boys playing tricks?" asked Ms. Colman.

Sam held up his hands. "It was not us." The Three Musketeers waited with Ms. Colman while Sam and his friends searched the house. They did not find anything.

Soon Nancy's mommy came to pick her

up. Nancy ran through the rain to Mrs. Dawes's car.

Sam walked Hannie and me home. It was still drizzling. I was cold and wet and miserable by the time we reached the big house. As we passed Morbidda Destiny's, I could see warm yellow lights on inside. Smoke was curling up from their chimney. I pictured Druscilla and Mrs. Porter in the kitchen, stirring a big cauldron. (And Mrs. Peterson, Druscilla's mom, if she were a witch too. And she probably was. Daddy had said she was a lawyer, but that did not mean she was not a witch in her spare time.)

I was convinced that somehow Druscilla was behind the hauntings of the haunted house. I could think of two reasons she would want to do something mean to me. One, *I* had said mean things to *her*. Two, I wanted her to give up being Cinderella for Halloween. But how could I prove Druscilla was trying to scare me?

11

Halloween Problems

I will show her, I thought. I will show Druscilla that she should leave being Cinderella to someone who *really* knows how to be Cinderella.

On Sunday I did not go to the haunted house to decorate. Our room was almost finished, and I wanted to work on my Halloween costume. Now I was in my room, trying on my fake glass slippers and my gown and my cape with the fake fur.

I looked gigundoly wonderful. Elizabeth's old party dress fit me perfectly. It was lovely. My slippers looked like real glass slippers. And the cape was just the right touch. But I was not finished. I would have to do something with my hair. I decided to ask Kristy to give me a princessy hairdo on Halloween.

What else did I need? I thought back to the movie. Cinderella had a fancy necklace. I searched through my jewelry box and found a very fancy necklace with crystal beads on it. Perfect! And gloves. I needed fancy white party gloves. I remembered seeing some in the back of one of my drawers. They were behind my old, too small bathing suit.

My fake glass slippers had little heels on them, and I practiced walking. I decided I would have to wear tights with them, to be warm.

There was no doubt about it. I would be the best Cinderella on Halloween night.

"Karen, dinner," called Nannie from downstairs.

Oh, boy! I realized I was starving. Working on my costume had used up a lot of energy. I peeled off my costume and ran downstairs. I raced into the kitchen and grabbed a place next to Kristy.

"I am so huungryyyy," I sang. "Hungry is whaaat I am. There is nooobody as huungggryyyyy as me."

Nannie smiled at me. "Good. I hope you are ready for spaghetti and meatballs."

"Yum!" I said. Nannie piled my plate high.

"Speaking of spaghetti and meatballs," said Sam, "they kind of look like brains. Maybe I could use them at the haunted house."

Charlie swirled some spaghetti on his fork. "You are right," he said. "It does look like brains. And we all know your classmates could use some more brains."

Sam snorted. "You are just jealous," he said. "Because our room is so much scarier than your room. And because my costume is so much cooler than your costume. And because I have sold more tickets to the haunted house than you have."

"What?" cried Charlie. "You are dreaming. Your room is totally lame. Your costume stinks. And I have sold way more tickets than you."

"You have not!" said Sam.

"Have too!" said Charlie.

Elizabeth sighed and tapped her spoon against her water glass. "Stop it, you two. I do not know what the matter is with you lately. You have been bickering over everything. Now just be quiet for the rest of dinner, please."

Sam glared at Charlie. Charlie glared at Sam. I ate my spaghetti and meatballs. It was nice not being the one told to be quiet, for a change.

"So, I have bought two bat houses," said Daddy cheerfully. "I hung them on the back of the garage."

"What?" I cried. "Already? Why don't you just put up a sign saying 'Witches Welcome Here'? We do not want *bats* in — "

"Good, Watson," said Elizabeth loudly. "The bats will help keep insects away. And

they will not bother anyone during the day."
She smiled at Daddy.

"But — " I began.

"How many bats will two houses hold?"
interrupted Kristy.

"They are small houses, but each one will
hold between twenty and thirty bats," said
Daddy. "I guess the bats snuggle up inside."

I did not say anything for the rest of dinner. Afterward I went to my room, feeling
very grumpy. This Halloween was not turning out as I had hoped. Number one: Someone was haunting the haunted house.
(Druscilla, I thought.) Number two: There
would be two Cinderellas. (Druscilla again.)
Number three: Bats would live in the yard
at the big house. (Daddy.)

Would anything go right for me on Halloween?

12

The Last Straw

On Monday morning the three Musketeers met on the playground at school.

"We have to catch Druscilla in the act of haunting the haunted house," I said. "We must come up with a plan."

"If it *is* Druscilla," said Hannie.

"How could it not be Druscilla?" I asked.

"I mean, if it is a real ghost, instead," explained Hannie.

I did not like to think about it being a real ghost. I wanted it to be Druscilla.

"How could we catch a real ghost?" asked

Nancy. She frowned. "I do not even think I want to."

"Me neither," said Hannie.

"Oh, I bet it is not a real ghost," I said. "I bet it is Druscilla. Now, let's each try to think up some plan to catch her. At lunchtime we will compare plans. Then we will know what to do."

I felt very grown-up saying that. There was only one small problem: I had no ideas for a plan myself.

As it turned out, Hannie and Nancy could not think of anything either. We decided to think some more.

That afternoon our class went back to the haunted house. There was some work left to do, but not too much. The school bus dropped off Hannie, Nancy, Ms. Colman, Ricky, Sara, Leslie Morris, Bobby, Natalie, and me.

As we were trooping up the stairs to our

room, kids from both Sam's and Charlie's classes arrived too.

Sam pushed open the door to his class's room.

Whoosh! I turned around just in time to see a red plastic bucket fall onto Sam's head. The bucket was full of fireplace ashes! When Sam grabbed the bucket off his head, he looked as if he had been rolling in a fireplace. Soot and ashes covered his hair and face and shoulders and sweatshirt. His wide, surprised eyes stared whitely from his face.

"Oh, my goodness," said Ms. Colman.

Across the hall, Charlie started laughing. "You look like a ghost," he said. "A ghost in reverse."

"You did this!" said Sam angrily.

"I did not!" said Charlie. "How would I know you would be the one to open the door?" He chuckled again. "You *do* look pretty funny, though."

"Oh, ha, ha," said Sam.

Still chuckling, Charlie backed up to his class's door and pushed it open. *Whoosh!* A plastic bucket of ashes dropped down on *his* head!

He pulled the bucket off, and he looked just like Sam: all gray and black and sooty, with big white eyes.

Sam stared at him in disbelief, then doubled over with laughter. "You are right!" he said, gasping. "You do look funny that way!"

"Okay, this has gone far enough, boys," said Sam's teacher. "I do not know who is responsible, but let's get this mess cleaned up. We still have work to do. We do not have time for pranks."

"All right, class," said Ms. Colman to my friends and me. "The show is over. Let's go to our own room, please."

I headed toward our room. Either Druscilla had sneaked in and put the buckets of ashes over the doorways, or . . . it was a real ghost. I did not like to think about it.

I turned the handle on our door and

started to open it. *Whoosh!* A plastic bucket of ashes and soot fell down on *my* head! "Ew!" I cried. I tasted ashes in my mouth!

Ms. Colman grabbed the bucket off my head. "Karen, are you all right?" she asked.

I blinked. I was covered with yucky, dirty, fireplace ashes. They were in my hair. They were down my shirt. They were all over my face. I took off my glasses and blinked again. My classmates were staring at me. Hannie's mouth dropped open. Nancy had covered her face with her hands. Ms. Colman took my glasses and wiped them off.

For a moment I felt tears come to my eyes. This was one of the worst things that had ever happened to me. I was so embarrassed. Everyone was staring at me. Then I had one thought: Druscilla. Druscilla has gone too far.

13

Druscilla's Alibi

"I am all right," I said, but my voice wavered.

"I cannot believe this happened," said Hannie.

"I wish I had thought of it," said Bobby.

"Since you live right down the street, Karen, why don't you go home and get cleaned up?" said Ms. Colman kindly. "You do not have to come back today if you do not feel like it."

"Okay," I said. But I had another plan. I had something to do *before* I went home. Under the ashes, my face was burning with embarrassment. I felt terrible. But I was going to do something about it.

"I will come with you," said Hannie. She patted my shoulder, then looked at her fingers and wiped them on her jeans.

"I will come too," said Nancy.

"I guess that would be all right," said Ms. Colman. "Be sure to come right back, though."

We left the haunted house. (Hannie told her mother why we were leaving.)

"You will probably want to take a shower," said Nancy, looking at the trail of ashes floating behind me.

"Yes," I said. "But first I am going to let Druscilla have it."

"Druscilla?" asked Hannie.

"Yes." We crossed the street. "Druscilla was the one who put the buckets over the doors. I am sure of it. Now I am going to have a talk with her."

"Um," said Nancy. "Are you really sure?"

"I am positive." We stopped in front of

Mrs. Porter's house. I had been here only a few times before. It was very creepy, even in the daytime. I stepped up on the porch and rang the doorbell.

Morbidda Destiny herself answered the door. As usual, she was dressed all in black. Her frizzy gray hair stuck out like a cloud around her head. She peered at me.

"Karen, is that you?" she asked.

"Yes," I said. "I had an, um, accident. Is Druscilla here, please?"

"Yes. She is up in her room," said Mrs. Porter. "It is the second door on the left. I know she will be happy to see you."

I do not think so, I thought as we headed up the stairs.

Inside, Morbidda Destiny's house looked pretty much like any other house. Tables, lamps, chairs. Their witchy things were probably hidden in the basement. I felt angry all over again.

I stomped down the hall and knocked on the second door on the left. Then I flung open the door.

"Listen, Druscilla Peterson," I began. Then I stopped. Druscilla was in her nightgown, sitting up in bed. A box of tissues was next to her. She was reading a magazine. Bottles of medicine stood on her bedside table. Her nose was red and puffy. She stared at me in surprise, then sneezed and grabbed a tissue.

"What happedd to you?" she asked. She sounded very stuffy-nosy.

"Um, how long have you been sick?" I asked.

"All weekedd," she said. "Dot that you care."

Well, for heaven's sake.

Mrs. Porter followed us into Druscilla's room. "Yes, poor thing," she said. "She came down with it Friday night. She's been in bed ever since. Now, can I get you girls some juice? Or do you, ah, need to get cleaned up?"

I remembered that I was covered with soot. "I better go get cleaned up," I said meekly.

"Thank you, anyway," said Hannie.

"We hope you feel better, Druscilla," said Nancy.

I slunk out of the room and down the stairs. We told Mrs. Porter good-bye. Hannie and Nancy walked me home, and then they headed back to the haunted house. I felt worse than ever.

14

The Apology

If you have never been covered with soot and ashes, you might not know that it takes about three showers to get really clean again. Well, it does. I had to shampoo and shampoo and shampoo my hair. Then I put on clean clothes. I lay on my bed and thought.

Druscilla had been very sick all weekend. She had not been faking it. So she could not have done the spooky things at the haunted house. And she could not have set up the buckets of ashes.

So who *had* done those things? Was the house really haunted? I did not know. But one thing was clear: I owed Druscilla an apology.

After dinner I asked Daddy if I could go next door for a minute. Also if I could pick some of his mums from the garden.

"Yes, I suppose so," said Daddy. "But do not be gone too long."

So for the second time that day I climbed the steps to Morbidda Destiny's porch. It was dark outside. I shivered. What if the witches were in the middle of casting a spell? I rang the doorbell. A small black shape ran by my legs, and I almost screamed. But it was just Midnight, Morbidda Destiny's black cat. (Witches always have black cats.)

Mrs. Porter opened the door. She smiled at me. "Well, you look much more like yourself," she said.

"Thank you," I said. "May I see Druscilla again, please?"

Up in Druscilla's room I gave her the

flowers. She looked at me suspiciously.

"I owe you an apology," I said. (I hate apologizing. But it is very necessary sometimes.) "I am sorry I accused you of haunting the haunted house. It was haunted all last weekend, and today too, and now I know you could not have done it."

"Hauted how?" asked Druscilla.

So I told her everything that had been happening.

"Ooh, that souds spooky," she said. "Could it have bid Sab or Charlie?"

"Sam is a practical joker, but he got ashes dumped on him too," I said.

"Baybe he did that just to throw people off the track," said Druscilla. She sniffled.

"Maybe. But he looked really mad," I said.

"Baybe it was Bobby," said Druscilla. "You said he threw a spider at you."

I nodded. I needed to think about all the evidence.

"I also need to apologize for telling you you cannot be Cinderella," I said. "It is not a problem if we are both Cinderella."

"No, of course dot," said Druscilla. She blew her nose. "I ab sure we will look differedt, adyway."

"Yes," I said. "There is no way we could come up with the exact same costume." Druscilla and I chatted for awhile longer. She said she had been very lonely and bored all weekend. The kids at Stoneybrook Day School were nice, but she had not made many real friends yet.

I decided again to try to be friends with Druscilla.

Finally I went back home. Druscilla had promised to come help decorate the haunted house when she was better. Maybe with her help, we would get to the bottom of our ghost mystery.

15

Sam or Charlie?

"Okay, if it is not Druscilla, then maybe it is Sam or Charlie or Bobby," I said on Tuesday at recess.

Hannie pushed herself slowly in the swing. "Or a real ghost," she said.

"Well, yeah," I said. "Or a real ghost."

"I think it is Sam or Charlie," said Nancy. "I do not want it to be a real ghost."

"Me neither," I said. "A real ghost will be much harder to catch. But I have a plan for catching Sam or Charlie. Or Bobby. Listen."

The other two Musketeers leaned forward

while I whispered my plan to them. We agreed to try it the next day. We were going to be ghostbusters!

"Our room is almost finished," said Ms. Colman. "There is very little left to do. Today is Wednesday. We will work today and by Thursday, we will be completely done. On Friday, if you want to see the bats, come at dusk. That is the time they leave the house each day. And Friday is the day they will go off to their new homes.

"Eww," I said.

"Meanwhile, Bobby should finish the closet," said Ms. Colman. "Karen, Hannie, and Nancy can set the table with our skeleton-party refreshments. Sara and Audrey can sprinkle more dust around, especially in the corners. Any questions?"

No one had questions.

"Remember our plan," I whispered to Hannie and Nancy as we gathered our supplies. They nodded. Today was the second-to-last chance we had to catch the spook.

Sam's class had already finished their room, so Sam was not at the house. But we could still investigate our other suspects.

In the meantime, the Three Musketeers got to work. We tried to make the refreshments table as yucky as possible. We had a bag of gummy worms, and we put them all over the fake food. It looked disgusting.

"I am glad we do not have to eat this," said Hannie.

"If a skeleton eats something, can you see it in its bones?" asked Nancy.

"Eww!" I said, giggling. "That is so, so gross."

"I bet you can," said Bobby. "I bet you can see everything."

"Yuck!" I said. Then I bit part of a gummy worm and let the other half of it hang out of my mouth. I stuck my hands out in front, as if I were a zombie. "Agh," I said in a deep voice. I staggered around the room, staring at nothing. "Agh."

Hannie and Nancy laughed, and so did Bobby.

Suddenly the lights went out!

"*Aiiee!*" screamed Nancy. Audrey screamed too.

It was practically dark outside, so it was *very* dark inside our room. But there was enough light for me to see Bobby standing still, looking scared. So, Bobby was not our ghost. There was no way he could have turned out the lights from where he stood.

"Everyone, please stay calm," said Ms. Colman. "I am sure it is just a fuse, and it will be fixed in a moment."

"Quick," I whispered. "Our plan!"

Hannie and Nancy and I sneaked over to the door and opened it. The hallway was very dark, but we could see a little bit.

Two doors down, Charlie came out of his room. Several of his classmates were with him. "What is going on?" he said. He sounded cross.

I looked at Hannie and Nancy. "It must be Sam," I said, and they nodded.

The lights flashed back on. I blinked for a

moment, then ran for the stairs. "Come on!" I called. "Let's catch him!"

The haunted house had one old phone, in the kitchen. I ran to it and called the big house. Nannie answered.

"Nannie, is Sam there?" I asked. When Nannie said he was not, I gave Hannie and Nancy a thumbs-up. I covered the phone with my hand. "It *is* him! He is not at home! He must have snuck over here!"

Then Nannie said, "Oh, here he is now, with the groceries. I asked him to pick up a few things. I better go help him unload them."

I hung up the phone. I did not know what to think. "Sam was at the grocery store," I told Hannie and Nancy. "He just came home."

"With real groceries?" asked Hannie suspiciously.

"Yes," I said. I felt very disappointed.

16

Charlie or Sam?

The ghost was not Bobby. Sam had been at the grocery store. The Three Musketeers decided it must have been Charlie somehow, but we did not know how. We would have to keep an extra-careful watch on him.

Thursday was our last day at the haunted house. Druscilla was finally over her cold, and she came to help with last-minute details. We gave her a tour of our room. She had probably seen creepier things in her own house, but she acted very impressed.

"And here is a creepy closet," I said, opening the door. Bobby had rigged the door so that when it opened, spiders on elastic strings dropped down. Plus there were glow-in-the-dark skeletons painted inside.

"Ooh," said Druscilla.

"And here is our blood punch," said Hannie. We had filled a punch bowl with Hawaiian Punch and then added more red food coloring to it. It looked just like blood.

"Bleah," said Druscilla, wrinkling her nose. I watched her nose carefully, to see if she was casting spells with it. She did not seem to be.

"And here are our dancing skeletons," Nancy said. Ms. Colman had cut several skeletons out of light tissue paper. We had hung them on threads from the ceiling. A crack in the window let in a breeze, making them look as if they were dancing.

"Creepy," said Druscilla. "This room is really great."

I smiled at Druscilla. I could not forget that she was going to be Cinderella too, but otherwise she was pretty nice. For a W.I.T.

"I am sorry to hear that your plan did not catch the ghost yesterday," Druscilla said quietly. "I really thought it would work."

"Me too," I said. "Today if anything happens, we are going to stick to Charlie like glue."

Just then, over our heads, heavy footsteps thumped back and forth. We heard the scrape and clanking of metal chains. We heard a voice wail, *"Whoooooooo!"* and then a creepy laugh: *"Ha-ha-ha-ha-haaaa!"*

Druscilla looked at the ceiling, her eyes wide. "Something like that?" she asked, pointing upward. "Someone is in the attic!"

"Charlie!" my friends and I yelled. Then we tore down the hall to Charlie's room. Charlie was not there.

"Aha!" I cried. "It is definitely him!"

"Definitely who?" asked Charlie from behind me.

I was not expecting to see him there, and I yelled. *"Aaaugh!"*

Charlie held up a can of paint. "I was get-

ting more paint," he said. "What are you all doing out here?"

"There is someone in the attic," I said.

"Or some*thing*," said Hannie.

"Let's go see," said Charlie.

Mrs. Papadakis had blocked off the attic stairs with ropes so that people would not go up to the attic. But we ducked under the ropes: Charlie first, then the Three Musketeers, then Druscilla.

"No one has been up here," said Charlie. "Look at the steps."

Sure enough, the attic steps were covered with a thick layer of dust. It had not been disturbed.

"Let's go up anyway," I said bravely.

We climbed the steps slowly, with Charlie in the lead. After all, he was the biggest.

Charlie opened the little door at the top of the stairs. He felt around on the wall for a light switch and flicked it on. I leaned past Charlie and looked into the attic.

Then I gasped.

17

There Is a Ghost!

You will find this hard to believe. (I did.) But it's true: All over the floor of the attic, there were footprints in the dust. *Even though there had been no footprints on the attic stairs.*

"Is there another door?" asked Druscilla.

We all looked, but we could see only one door, the one we had come in.

"How did someone get in here without coming up the stairs?" asked Nancy.

"They *floated* in," said Hannie. Her voice shook.

That did it. We stared at each other, then we all yelled and leaped for the door. With all of us pushing to get out, we caused a traffic jam, which just made us push harder. I was terrified that a ghost would clamp a cold hand on my shoulder, right then and there.

Finally, with a little *"Oof!"* we managed to burst through the doorway. We thundered down the steps to the second floor. Ms. Colman was waiting for us at the bottom.

"Girls, you are not supposed to go into the attic," she said. "We are not sure it is safe."

"It is definitely *not* safe!" I said. Charlie, Druscilla, Hannie, and Nancy nodded their heads. We had solved the mystery. The ghost was real.

"That was so spooky," said Hannie.

The Three Musketeers and Druscilla were sitting at the kitchen table in the big house. We were still shaken up. Nannie had fixed us some emergency hot apple cider. We each had our own cinnamon stick.

I nodded and reached for a ginger snap. "It was just about the spookiest thing I have ever seen," I said.

"It could not have been Charlie," said Nancy.

"It was not Bobby or Sam," I said.

"It was not me," said Druscilla, smiling.

I smiled back at her. "No, it was definitely not you."

"It was something that can float up stairs," said Hannie. She shivered just thinking about it.

"If it floated up the stairs, why did it leave footprints in the attic?" asked Nancy. "Why didn't it just float around the attic?"

"It *had* to walk around in the attic," explained Hannie. "Because it had to make a lot of noise to scare people."

I put my head in my hands. My plan to catch Sam or Charlie had backfired. I had almost ended up catching a real ghost. Or a real ghost had almost caught me! I decided that I would forget about catching anything. I would try to enjoy the haunted house anyway, and leave the ghost alone. But . . . would the ghost leave *me* alone?

18

Going Batty

This Halloween was turning out to be the Halloweeniest ever. Not only had I found a real ghost, but something else was spooky: Daddy's new bat friends.

I had looked at the two new bat houses on the back of the garage. They looked just like small, plain wooden boxes. I could not see a door anywhere. Daddy explained that the bottom was open. The bats would fly in from the bottom, then cling upside down inside the box. I wrinkled my nose. What kind of creepy animal would sleep upside down? Only a witchy bat, of course.

On Friday evening before dinner, my big-house family walked down the street to the haunted house. It was a cool, clear night. A fat, pale moon was just starting to rise. The sky was not completely dark yet.

Many people had gathered around the haunted house. Mrs. Porter and Druscilla were there, along with Druscilla's mother.

"Welcome, everyone," said Mrs. Porter. "I want to thank you for your support of one of nature's most misunderstood animals, the bat." She talked about how bats are good for eating insects, and how people do not have to be afraid of bats.

Sure, I thought.

Then she talked about how they planned to save the haunted-house bats.

"In just a few minutes the bats will swarm out of the chimney," said Mrs. Porter. "Once they are out on their nightly insect raid, an animal-control worker will cover the chimney opening with netting. When the bats realize they cannot return home, they will look for new homes. Many of you have installed bat houses in your yards. If you have baited them with fruit, bats will find them and move into them very quickly. In just a day or two I hope that all of our lovely bats will have new homes."

The crowd clapped their hands. I sighed. I did not want bats living behind our garage.

"Oh, look!" Elizabeth said. "There they are now."

We looked up to the roof of the haunted house. Dozens of dark little creatures were flying out of the chimney. They did not make any sound. They looked like small brown birds.

I shivered and grabbed Daddy's hand. I pressed close to his sweater. If a bat came after me, I wanted Daddy to protect me.

"There must be hundreds of them," said Daddy. "I am glad we will be able to help some of them with our bat houses."

"I think they are neat," said Kristy.

I watched the bats as they flew away

through the night. I still did not think they were neat, or lovely. But at least none of them had swooped down to attack me. And at least they slept all day. I probably would not run into any bats soon. That is how I wanted to keep it.

19

Will the Real Ghost Please Stand Up?

"There. How is that?" asked Kristy.

I stood back and looked at myself in the mirror. Kristy had fixed my hair in a very fancy princessy hairdo.

"It is wonderful!" I said. "Thank you, Kristy."

"No problem. Can you put on the rest of your costume while I help Andrew?"

"Yes," I said. It was Halloween afternoon. Kristy had agreed to take Hannie, Nancy, Andrew, Druscilla, and me trick-or-treating in the neighborhood. Then we would go to the haunted house together around five o'clock. I could not wait.

Soon we were standing in front of Druscilla's house while Kristy rang the doorbell. Andrew had decided to be a dinosaur this year. Hannie was a butterfly. Nancy was a pumpkin. And I, of course, was Cinderella.

Kristy came down the steps. (She was dressed as the bride of Frankenstein's monster.) Druscilla was right behind her. When I saw her, my eyes opened wide. Then I started to laugh.

Druscilla and I did not look anything alike! I was Cinderella *after* she had become a beautiful princess. Druscilla was Cinderella *before* her fairy godmother had made her beautiful. Druscilla was dressed in a too-small, raggedy dress with tears and rips in it. She had smeared dirt on her face. Her hair was wild and uncombed. She looked as if she had been scrubbing floors all day. I had been worried for nothing.

"You look great!" I said happily.

"You look great too!" said Druscilla.

"Let's trick-or-treat!" I cried.

Kristy waited for us at each house. Slowly our plastic pumpkin buckets filled with candy.

"Yea!" Andrew cheered as two more Tootsie Rolls dropped into his bucket.

"We will have to sort it all out later," I said. "Mommy will let us have only two pieces a day."

"My mom lets me eat it all at once," said Nancy.

"Maybe we can have a sleepover at your house," I said. "Then we could eat more candy."

"Good idea," said Hannie. "My mom makes me save my candy too."

"Okay," said Nancy. "I will ask."

After we had gone to most of the houses in our neighborhood, it was time to visit the haunted house. We turned the corner onto our street. First we stopped off at my house and dropped off our plastic pumpkins. Then we headed down the street to the haunted house.

104

"Gee, look at that," said Hannie.

There was a long line in front of the haunted house. It went halfway down the street!

"It looks like a big success," said Kristy.

"We will raise a lot of money for Homes for Families," said Hannie.

"Look," I said. "There are even some television news teams. Our haunted house might be on the news tonight!"

I wanted to hang around outside, in case any of the newspeople needed to interview someone who had worked on the house. But everyone else wanted to go in. I was outvoted.

I felt very important as we passed the long line of people waiting to get in. (We could skip ahead because we were not customers.)

Inside, the house was even spookier than it had been on Thursday. Andrew decided the house was *too* scary for him, so Kristy offered to take him home. She would come back for us later.

The four of us walked through the house slowly. It was hard to believe that we had helped make it look so scary. Even though we had seen it all happen from the beginning, we still jumped when things leaped out at us. The scary music and sound effects were still creepy. We still grabbed each other's hands when lights flickered and ghosts wailed. Just thinking about the *real* ghost upstairs made everything twice as spooky.

"This is great!" said Hannie.

We were on the second floor, looking at the bedrooms. Both Sam's and Charlie's rooms were very scary. One of Charlie's classmates pretended to be stuck in the giant spiderweb. He was all tangled up in the ropes. It looked as if the big (fake) spider were going to get him. I hoped I would not have bad dreams about it.

"Everyone did a great job," said Nancy.

"I think your room is best," said Druscilla. "I am glad you were able to finish it, even though the house was haunted while you were working."

"Thank you," I said. Then I had a sudden thought. Earlier I had decided not to try to catch the ghost after all. But now that we were in the haunted house on Halloween night, it was too good a chance to pass up.

"Uh-oh," said Nancy, looking at me. "I know that face. Karen is about to make us do something we do not want to do."

"It is a great idea," I said. "But it is scary. But we should do it. But you might not want to. But I hope you do."

"This sounds bad," said Hannie.

"Look," I said quickly. "The house was haunted while we were working on it. It must still be haunted. And this is Halloween night. If the ghost is going to do something really spooky, it will be tonight."

"I do not like the way you are thinking," said Nancy.

"We should go up to the attic," I went on. "We will hide up there quietly. Then we will be able to see the ghost when it begins to haunt the house. We will all be together, so we will be safe."

"This is a bad idea," said Nancy.

"I will do it," said Druscilla.

"Me too," said Hannie. "If we are all together."

"Well, I will not stay down here by myself," said Nancy.

So we slipped under the rope across the attic stairs. We crept up the stairs and slowly opened the door. The attic was quiet and dark. A beam of moonlight shone through the attic window. We did not turn on the electric light. Quietly we hid behind a pile of old furniture. And we waited.

20

Happy Halloween!

I hoped we would not have to wait long. The four of us huddled together. We decided, in whispers, that we would just run for the door if we got too scared.

"Shh!" Hannie said quietly.

A cold shiver went down my back. Across the attic, a door slowly creaked open. Not the door we had come in — a hidden door! One we had not seen earlier. I bit my knuckles. It was the ghost! We were about to catch the ghost at last!

Someone — or something — crept through the door.

"Do ghosts usually carry flashlights?" Druscilla breathed in my ear.

I frowned. No, ghosts usually do not carry flashlights, I thought. They are ghosts. They can see in the dark. I squinted hard, looking at the figure. Then my eyes widened. I recognized that costume. I had seen it just a few hours earlier, at the big house. It was Sam. Sam was the ghost after all!

I was about to leap up and accuse Sam of haunting the house when Hannie grabbed my arm. She pointed to the other door, the one we had come in. It was opening too. I saw Sam quickly hide. Someone with a flashlight sneaked in through the other door. It was getting crowded up here!

Just then Sam leaped out and flicked on the light switch. I saw Charlie standing there, frozen. Well, for heaven's sake.

"You!" Sam shouted. "I knew it was you!"

"Me?" cried Charlie. "It was you! You were behind all the tricks!"

Then I leaped out from behind the furniture, with Hannie, Nancy, and Druscilla behind me. "It was both of you!" I cried.

My brothers looked shocked. Sam even leaned against the wall with his hand over his heart.

"Admit it," I said, with my hands on my hips. "It was both of you."

Sam and Charlie glared at each other. I glared at both of them. Then Sam's mouth crinkled at the corners. Charlie's eyes twinkled. First Sam, then Charlie started smiling, and then chuckling, and then laughing.

I could not help it. I started laughing too.

When we had all finished laughing, Sam and Charlie admitted they had each played some of the pranks. Each one was trying to scare the other's class. They had not meant to scare me or my class, but it had happened anyway.

It turned out that Sam had found the secret door to the attic. So he had made all the weird attic sounds.

Charlie had made the other eerie noises.

111

He had found speaking tubes in the walls. In the old days, people would use them to talk to their servants on different floors. The tubes were well hidden, so we never saw where the spooky wailing was coming from.

It was just chance that they had each thought of putting a bucket of ashes over the other's doorway.

"Yes, but which one of you put the bucket of ashes over *my* doorway?" I asked. "It was not very funny at all."

Charlie frowned. "I did not do that, Karen," he said. "I promise. I would not do that to you."

"It was not me either," Sam said, holding up his hands. "I would not pick on a second-grader."

I narrowed my eyes. "Well, then, who did it? Those ashes made a gigundo mess. I had to wash my hair three times. You should apologize."

"I would apologize if I had done it," said Charlie. "But I did not. Cross my heart and hope to die." He crossed his heart.

"I swear that I did not do it," said Sam.

I looked from one to the other. They both seemed very innocent. I did not know what to think. If they had not done it, who had?

"I guess it is just a Halloween mystery," said Nancy.

"Maybe there is a real ghost after all," said Hannie. She looked around the attic suspiciously.

"Well, let's go downstairs and join the party," I said. "I will get to the bottom of this someday."

Sam and Charlie pounded down the attic steps ahead of us. They were bickering again.

"Your ghost noises were so lame," said Sam.

"Your chain rattling was for babies," said Charlie.

I grinned at Hannie and Nancy. Things were back to normal. Then, out of the corner of my eye, I saw Druscilla. She looked very innocent. Almost *too* innocent. All of a sudden I saw her nose twitch.

Uh-oh!

L. GODWIN

About the Author

ANN M. MARTIN lives in New York City and loves animals, especially cats. She has two cats of her own, Gussie and Woody.

Other books by Ann M. Martin that you might enjoy are *Stage Fright*; *Me and Katie (the Pest)*; and the books in *The Baby-sitters Club* series.

Ann likes ice cream and *I Love Lucy*. And she has her own little sister, whose name is Jane.

Little Sister

Don't miss #91

KAREN'S PILGRIM

Pamela said, "I want to show all my Plimoth Plantation souvenirs."

"Could you please not show the marbles or pen-and-ink set? Those are the things I am going to present," I said.

"Yoo bad again," said Pamela. "Why should I not show them when I have them?"

"Because you have the poppet doll. That is special enough," I replied.

"But my presentation will be more special with *all* my souvenirs," said Pamela. She turned and walked straight to Ms. Colman's desk.

I was so mad. If Pamela showed all her souvenirs, that would leave nothing special for me. And Pamela's presentation was on Monday. Mine was not until Tuesday. Who would want to see the same things twice?

It was no fair!

BABY-SITTERS™
Little Sister
by Ann M. Martin
author of The Baby-sitters Club®

More Titles... ➡

♥ ♥

The Baby-sitters Little Sister titles continued...

- -

Available wherever you buy books, or use this order form.

Scholastic Inc., P.O. Box 7502, Jefferson City, MO 65102

Please send me the books I have checked above. I am enclosing $_____
(please add $2.00 to cover shipping and handling). Send check or money order – no
cash or C.O.Ds please.

Name_____ Birthdate_____.

Address_____

City_____ State/Zip_____

Please allow four to six weeks for delivery. Offer good in U.S.A. only. Sorry, mail orders are not available to residents to Canada. Prices subject to change.   BSLS497

♥ ♥

LITTLE 🍎 APPLE®

Here are some of our favorite Little Apples.

There are fun times ahead with kids just like you in Little Apple books! Once you take a bite out of a Little Apple—you'll want to read more!

Reading Excitement for Kids with BIG Appetites!

☐	NA45899-X	**Amber Brown Is Not a Crayon** Paula Danziger $2.99
☐	NA93425-2	**Amber Brown Goes Fourth** Paula Danziger $2.99
☐	NA50207-7	**You Can't Eat Your Chicken Pox, Amber Brown** Paula Danziger $2.99
☐	NA42833-0	**Catwings** Ursula K. LeGuin $2.95
☐	NA42832-2	**Catwings Return** Ursula K. LeGuin $3.50
☐	NA41821-1	**Class Clown** Johanna Hurwitz $2.99
☐	NA42400-9	**Five True Horse Stories** Margaret Davidson $2.99
☐	NA43868-9	**The Haunting of Grade Three** Grace Maccarone $2.99
☐	NA40966-2	**Rent a Third Grader** B.B. Hiller $2.99
☐	NA41944-7	**The Return of the Third Grade Ghost Hunters** Grace Maccarone $2.99
☐	NA42031-3	**Teacher's Pet** Johanna Hurwitz $3.50

Available wherever you buy books...or use the coupon below.

SCHOLASTIC INC., P.O. Box 7502, 2931 East McCarty Street, Jefferson City, MO 65102

Please send me the books I have checked above. I am enclosing $ _____ (please add $2.00 to cover shipping and handling). Send check or money order—no cash or C.O.D.s please.

Name_____

Address_____

City_____State/Zip_____

Please allow four to six weeks for delivery. Offer good in the U.S.A. only. Sorry, mail orders are not available to residents of Canada. Prices subject to change.

LA996